5629 1833

W9-AHM-384

WITHDRAWN

BEAVERTON CITY LIBRARY
Beaverton, OR 97005
Member of Washington County
COOPERATIVE LIBRARY SERVICES

Dear Parents,

ASPCA Rescue Readers series tells stories of animal adoptions from the animal's point of view! Written with warmth and gentle humor, these leveled texts are designed to support young readers in their growth while connecting to their passion for pets.

Level 2 in this series is designed for early readers who need short simple sentences, familiar vocabulary, informative illustrations, and easier spelling patterns to give them support as they practice to become fluent readers.

When you're reading with your children, you can help by encouraging them to think about using more than one strategy to unlock new words. Successful readers solve words in a variety of ways. Here are some tips you might share with your child:

 Take a picture walk before you read so you can preview the story.

 Sound out the word, remembering that some letters say more than one sound.

 For long words, cover up the end so you can figure out the beginning first.

 Check the picture to see if it gives you some clues.

 Skip over the word and read a little further along. Then come back to it.

Think about what is happening in this story. What would make sense here?

Learning to read is an exciting moment in a child's life. A wonderful way to share in that moment is to have conversations about the books after reading. Children love talking about their favorite part, or connecting the story to their own lives. I hope you'll enjoy sharing in the fun as your children get to know Daisy and all the other adopted pets that are part of this series. Happy reading!

Ellie Costa, M.S. Ed.
Literacy Specialist, Bank Street College of Education

Published by Studio Fun International, Inc.
44 South Broadway, White Plains, NY 10601 U.S.A. and
Studio Fun International Limited,
The Ice House, 124-126 Walcot Street, Bath UK BA1 5BG
Illustration © 2015 Studio Fun International, Inc.
Text © 2015 ASPCA®
All rights reserved.
Studio Fun Books is a trademark of Studio Fun International, Inc.,
a subsidiary of The Reader's Digest Association, Inc.
Printed in China.
Conforms to ASTM F963
10 9 8 7 6 5 4 3 2 1
SL1/09/14
***The American Society for the Prevention of Cruelty to Animals (ASPCA®) will
receive a minimum guarantee from Studio Fun International, Inc. of $25,000
for the sale of ASPCA® products through December 2017.
Comments? Questions? Call us at: 1-800-217-3346**

Library of Congress Cataloging-in-Publication Data

Froeb, Lori.
 I am Daisy / by Lori C. Froeb.
    pages cm -- (Rescue readers)
 Summary: "Meet Daisy the cat. She is so happy to be leaving the shelter
with all those loud dogs. Travel along with her as she meets her new
family, and discovers that 'Oh, no!' they have a dog too!" -- Provided by
publisher.
 ISBN 978-0-7944-3311-6 (paperback)
 1. Cats--Juvenile fiction. [1. Cats--Fiction. 2. Dogs--Fiction. 3. Pet
adoption--Fiction.] I. Title.
 PZ10.3.F9335Iad 2015
 [E]--dc23
                            2014030657

Hardcover ISBN 978-0-7944-3350-5

I Am Daisy

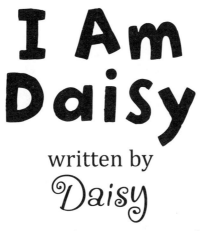

written by
Daisy

(with help from Lori C. Froeb)

illustrated by Violet Lemay

studio BOOKS

White Plains, New York • Montréal, Québec • Bath, United Kingdom

Meow!

I am Daisy.

Today is a very special day.
I am leaving the shelter!
I can't wait!

The shelter is full of dogs.

They bark and they bark.

Why can't they be quiet? Like me!

A cat can't get her beauty sleep around here.

Here is my new person.

Her name is Jen.

She is taking me home.

I met Jen a few days ago.

I could tell she was special.

I purred at her and she purred back.

I think she might speak cat!

Jen rubs behind my ears.

She says, "Jake and Henry can't wait to meet you!"

Jen is so nice.

I hope Jake and Henry are nice, too.

I am happy to be away from dogs!

I meet Jake first.

He can't wait to take me out of the car.

He tugs the carrier a little too hard.

I hiss because he scares me.

That scares him, too.

I meow and Jake laughs.

I wonder where Henry is.

We are at my new home.
I can't wait to nap on Jen's lap.

Wait a minute.

What is that smell?

What is that sound?

Oh, no. Henry is a DOG!

14

Henry puts his nose in my face.

I swat him!

Henry needs to know that I am the boss.

Henry yelps and sits with Jake.

Silly dog.

"Don't worry," Jen says.
"Daisy and Henry
will be friends soon."
I don't think so.

Henry stares at me from across the room.

That's good.

I like my space.

Wait! What's that?

Jake rolls a small ball.

I must chase it!

Henry chases it, too.

Henry bumps the ball to me.

Is Henry trying to be friends?

Cats and dogs can't be friends.

It *would* be nice to have a friend.

Before I lived at the shelter,

I lived with Mrs. Green.

She was too old to play.

We napped most of the time.

Mrs. Green got too old to take care of me.

That's when I went to the shelter.

I meow at Henry.

Maybe he can speak cat.

He yips back.

But his tail is wagging.

I think he wants to play!

I bat the ball back to Henry.

He catches it in his mouth.

Now there is slobber on it.

Dogs are gross.

This game is over.

Jen and Jake give me a special cat tree.

It is too tall for Henry to reach.

I think I'll give myself a bath.

I don't want to smell like dog.

I have a new dish and collar!
They both say Daisy.
I think about Mrs. Green.
She gave me the name Daisy.
It was the name of her favorite flower.

Jake rubs my head.

I love head rubs!

I give him a kitty head-bump.

Henry licks my paw.

It is kind of nice.

But now I need another bath.

I have learned a lot
since Jen brought me to her house.
That was months ago.
I sleep in all the warm spots.

I meow for Jake to give me treats.

And, now I know that cats and dogs
can be friends.

That's right!

Henry is okay for a dog.

He is a great playmate and pillow...

even when he snores.

Can you believe it?

I found the *purrrrfect* forever family!

But I wish I could teach them

how to speak cat!

Meet the real Daisy!

Daisy's owner surrendered her to a
rescue group when she could no longer
keep her. Daisy was lonely, but her loneliness
turned to joy when Jennifer found her and
brought her to her forever home. Jennifer
visited the shelter to look for a new companion
for her dog, Brandy, after Brandy's old
companion passed away. She saw Daisy and fell
in love. Today, Daisy and Brandy are the best of
friends and Jennifer calls the black-and-white
cat an angel—sent to show them love.

For more information on how to help animals,
go to **www.aspca.org/parents.**